Walt Disney's

BAMBI

WALT DISNEY'S

BAMBI

ADAPTED FROM THE FILM BY
Joanne Ryder

ILLUSTRATED BY
David Pacheco and Jesse Clay

DISNEY
PRESS

NEW YORK

FIRST EDITION
1 3 5 7 9 10 8 6 4 2

Library of Congress Catalog Card Number: 92-54876
ISBN: 1-56282-442-2 / 1-56282-443-0 (lib. bdg.)

Walt Disney's

BAMBI

CHAPTER ONE

One spring morning something wonderful was about to happen in the forest. But none of the woodland creatures knew just yet how special this morning would be.

In the gray dusk before dawn, the woods were quiet. Only the tall waterfall whispered steady and slow. An old owl, tired from hunting all night, glided on strong, silent wings back to his tree. A sleepy bird landed on his favorite branch, fluffed his feathers, and closed his eyes for a long day's rest.

As the sun crept into the sky, other creatures stirred. In the tall, towering trees, animals woke up. Long-tailed squirrels and tiny striped chipmunks uncurled and stretched. Morning was beginning, and it was time to look for breakfast.

A mother bird flew to her nest, carrying bright cherries for her three babies. Two of the young birds fought furiously over who would get the fruit. While they weren't looking, the third baby ate all the sweet cherries himself!

Near the ground, a tiny mouse crept from his round, grassy nest. Above his head a dewdrop trembled from a leaf. He caught the cool drop of water in his paws and washed his soft, furry face in dew.

A blue messenger bird, singing a new song, suddenly flew through the trees. Woodpeckers peeked from their tree holes to listen. Beavers popped up from the cool pond to hear. The messenger bird was spreading the news. Someone special had just been born!

As the blue bird passed overhead, all the woodland animals stopped what they were doing. Soon a trail of rabbits and quail, squirrels and chipmunks followed the bird through the forest.

Under Owl's tree, a young rabbit thumped on a hollow log with his broad, flat foot. Drumming was his way to call the animals.

"Wake up, friend Owl!" Thumper shouted to the sleeping bird.

"Oh, what now!" said Owl in a grumpy voice. He was still half-asleep.

Thumper didn't want Owl to miss the wonderful news. The little rabbit kept on drumming until Owl was wide awake.

"Hey! What's going on around here?" Owl asked, blinking and trying to make sense of all the excitement.

Below him a trail of animals was rushing by.

"It's happened, it's happened!" called Mother Rabbit as she dashed beneath the tree.

"The new prince is born!" the animals cried. "We're going to see him."

"Come on!" Thumper called to Owl. "You better hurry up."

As quick as he could, Owl followed the animals who were leaping and flying and dashing through the forest. All the curious creatures stopped at a thicket of bushes and peeked inside. Tucked in a safe, quiet space were two deer—a doe and her newborn fawn.

The fawn, covered with pale spots on his back, was fast asleep. He was lovely and small and very fragile looking.

"Well, this is quite an occasion!" said Owl to the new mother. "Yes, sir, it isn't every day a prince is born! You're to be congratulated."

"Yes, congratulations," said everyone, wishing her well.

The doe looked at all the animals who had come to admire her fawn. "Thank you very much," she said.

Then she gently nuzzled her baby to wake him.

"Come on," she said softly. "Wake up. We have company."

The young fawn opened his eyes, blinking at the brightness and all the smiling faces who called to him, "Hello! Hello, little prince!"

Old Owl grinned at him and called, "Yoo-hooooo," in a loud

voice. At first the fawn was startled, but Owl looked so funny with his big winking eyes that the fawn had to smile.

"Look! He's trying to get up," said Thumper.

Getting up was harder to do than the fawn had thought. His new long legs trembled and shook, and he crashed to the ground.

"A little wobbly, isn't he?" said the young rabbit.

"Thumper!" called his mother.

"Well, he is!" said Thumper. He had a habit of saying just what he thought, and it often got him into trouble.

"You *are* wobbly, aren't you," the little rabbit said again as the fawn tottered, then tumbled once more. His new legs were hard to control.

"Looks to me like he's getting a little sleepy," said Owl. "I think it's time we all left."

None of the animals wanted to leave, but Owl decided he knew what was best. He wouldn't take no for an answer, and he shooed them all away.

But not Thumper! The young rabbit was too curious to leave just yet. He lagged behind so he could watch the tiny yawning fawn a little longer.

"Thumper! Come on!" called his mother.

Thumper began to follow his brothers and sisters, but he stopped to ask the fawn's mother, "What are you going to call him?"

"I think I'll call him Bambi," she said.

"Hmmm, Bambi," said Thumper thoughtfully. "I guess that'll do all right."

Thumper ran off to join his family. He couldn't wait to tell them the new prince of the forest had a name—Bambi. This certainly *was* a morning to remember!

Nestled in the bushes, safe from harm, Bambi's mother gazed at the tiny fawn as he slept. "Bambi," she whispered. "My little Bambi."

While Bambi's mother sheltered her little fawn, someone else was watching over both of them. A noble stag stood on a tall cliff overlooking the thicket. He was a mighty and powerful deer, with broad antlers crowning his head. In the forest he was the Great Prince. On this special morning no one in the forest felt more joy than the proud stag as he stood admiring his new son—the young prince, Bambi.

CHAPTER TWO

Bambi soon discovered that the forest was a wonderful place to explore. Each day, his mother took him to new places in the woods. He tried to keep up with her, but it was so easy to fall behind. Bambi was curious about everything, and everyone was curious about him.

"Good morning!" called Mother Quail, leading a long line of children behind her.

Mother Quail and her babies ran around Bambi. There were so many of them that it was hard for Bambi to know whom to look at first.

"Good morning, Bambi! Good morning, young prince!" the quail chirped in their high, squeaky voices. Then they ran off, following their mother.

One little quail came back to take another peek at Bambi.

"Good-bye," she called, and then rushed away shyly.

Wherever Bambi went, animals greeted him from trees, bushes, and all sorts of places. "Good morning, young prince!" called a

voice. Bambi looked around to see who was speaking, but he didn't see anyone.

Then he looked up. Someone was hanging upside down from a branch! Bambi turned his head upside down to see her better. It was Mother Opossum and her three babies, hanging by their tails. How could they do that! Bambi wondered.

"Good morning, young prince!" the upside-down babies said.

Bambi turned away, amazed at all the different kinds of creatures there were in the woods.

Even the ground in the forest could do astonishing things. A bump in the ground was moving, and it was moving toward Bambi! The bump came closer and closer and then . . . pop! A mole popped out of his underground tunnel just in front of Bambi.

"Good morning!" said the busy mole to Bambi. He peeked up at the bright sky. "Humph! Nice sunny day!"

Before Bambi could respond in any way, the mole dashed back down into his tunnel and dug quickly away. How did the mole do that?

Bambi thought digging fast looked like fun. He wanted to move quickly, too, and he tried to run and scamper. Instead, his long legs tangled on some reeds, and he tripped.

His mother and the rabbit family found him lying on the ground.

Curious as always, Thumper asked, "Did the young prince fall down?"

"Is he hurt?" asked another rabbit.

"No, he's all right," Bambi's mother told them. She knew that running wasn't always easy for a fawn.

Running was very easy for Thumper, but it was not always easy for him to think before he spoke.

"He doesn't walk very good, does he?" Thumper asked.

"Thumper!" scolded his mama. "What did your father tell you this morning?"

His nose twitching uncomfortably, Thumper tried to remember. "If you can't say something nice," he said, "don't say nothing at all!" But that was a hard thing for a young talkative rabbit to do.

"Come on, Bambi, get up!" said his mother gently. "Try again."

Bambi tried once more, and all the rabbits hopped around, cheering for him.

"Come on! Get up, Bambi!" they called until he stood up at last. The rabbits giggled and led the way through the woods. As fast as he could, Bambi ran after them.

The young animals ran to a place where the ground sloped sharply. The rabbits had no trouble running down the slope, but it was too steep for Bambi. He couldn't walk down it on his legs, so he sat and slid all the way. The little fawn landed right in the middle of the rabbits. They giggled at him, and he smiled at them. Bambi was having fun playing with his new friends.

Quickly Thumper ran ahead and dashed into a hollow log. He thumped loudly on the log. *Thump. Thump. Thump.* Bambi and the other rabbits heard the sounds and found him.

"I'm thumping!" he told Bambi. "That's why they call me Thumper!"

His voice echoed through the hollow log. *"That's why they call me Thumper!"*

The echo startled him, and Thumper looked behind him to see if someone else was in the log repeating everything he said. He didn't see anyone.

"Thumper!" he yelled into the log.

"Thumper!" the echo called back.

Bambi and the rabbits laughed. There were many surprises for all of them in the woods today!

As he played with the rabbits, Bambi felt himself get stronger. He ran farther and faster. When they came to a fallen tree trunk, the rabbits leapt over it easily. But Bambi didn't know how to leap high enough to follow them.

"Come on," called Thumper, jumping onto the log. "You can do it.

"Hop over it—like this," said Thumper, trying to show him the way.

Bambi carefully watched Thumper hop. He was sure he could do that, too. He moved back and took a running leap, but deer and rabbits aren't built alike. Bambi's front legs made it over the log, but his back legs did not. He was stuck in the middle.

"You didn't hop far enough," said Thumper.

Bambi looked around at his hind legs. They were still on the wrong side of the log. He wished he could hop as well as Thumper, but he couldn't with his long legs. He would have to find his own way.

Bambi stretched one of his hind legs over the log.

"That's it," Thumper called, cheering him on. "Now the other one."

Bambi slipped his other leg over the log. He had made it across!

Bambi was so proud that he skipped ahead with the rabbits. But then he tumbled—and landed right on Thumper.

"Gee whiz! What happened that time?" asked Thumper.

Bambi didn't know. It seemed his legs still had a few surprises for him.

The young animals stopped to rest under a tree. Over their heads birds sang and flew from branch to branch, pecking at the hanging fruit.

What were these singing creatures? Bambi wondered. He looked to his friend Thumper for an explanation.

"Those are birds," said the little rabbit.

"Burr!" said Bambi.

"Look! He's trying to talk," Thumper called to the others.

"Burr!" repeated Bambi.

"He's trying to say *bird*," said another rabbit.

Thumper wanted to help his friend. "Say *bird*!" he told Bambi, wiggling his nose.

Bambi tried to imitate his friend. "Burr," he said, wiggling his nose.

"No," said Thumper, shaking his head. "Bur-duh!"

The birds flew around Bambi's face. "Say *bird*," they chirped.

So Bambi took a deep breath. "Bur-DUH!" he shouted in such a loud and strong voice that he blew some nearby birds away.

The rabbits were so excited, they ran to tell their mother and Bambi's mother what had happened.

"He talked! He talked!" Thumper cried.

"The young prince said *bird*!" called another rabbit.

Proud of himself, Bambi repeated his very first word again and again. "Bird, bird, bird, bird."

A small golden creature danced in midair in front of Bambi's eyes. Startled, Bambi watched as the dainty thing fluttered about his head. Delighted by its movements, Bambi chased the tiny flier as it darted quickly ahead and then danced in circles around him. It landed on Bambi's tail, as light as a feather.

The brightly colored creature had flown in the air like a bird, so Bambi called to it, "Bird!"

"No, that's not a bird," said Thumper. "That's a butterfly."

"Butterfly?" Bambi whispered. He turned around to look at it again, but the butterfly had flown away. Bambi thought he had found it, and, grinning, he leapt toward a patch of bright colors.

"Butterfly!" he cried at something golden and dainty.

Thumper laughed. "No, that's a flower!"

"Flower," repeated Bambi.

"Uh-huh," said Thumper, sitting in the flowers and sniffing one. "It's pretty!"

"Pretty," said Bambi, and he sniffed the flowers, too. Suddenly one of the flowers moved, and Bambi's nose touched the nose of a little skunk.

"Flower," called Bambi.

"Me?" said the skunk in surprise.

Thumper laughed and laughed.

"No, no, no," he cried. "That's not a flower. He's a little—"

But the young skunk interrupted. "Oh, that's all right," he said. "He can call me a flower if he wants to!" The little skunk giggled shyly. "I don't mind!"

"Pretty, pretty flower!" said Bambi.

"Ohhh, gosh," said the skunk, and he giggled softly again.

Bambi and Thumper ran off and played in the woods together until they heard a crash of thunder. Bold slashes of lightning lit the dark sky. A storm was coming.

"I think I'd better go home now," said Thumper quickly, and he dashed off to find his family.

Bambi found his mother, and they headed to their thicket, where they would be safe and dry. As she slept, the little fawn lay beside her, listening to the roaring skies. Tired from all his adventures, Bambi yawned, but he was still too curious to fall asleep right away. This was his first thunderstorm. Raindrops began falling, and they made soft pattering sounds as they landed on the leaves.

All through the woods other animals ran and flew toward their homes. As fast as she could, a squirrel raced up her tree and hid in her hole. A clever mouse ran from mushroom to mushroom trying to stay dry on the way back home. A mother bird flew to her nest and covered her babies with her warm wings. But the young birds were curious, too, and they looked out at the rainy woods.

Only the ducks and their ducklings enjoyed being out in the rain. It was a fine time for a duck to take a bath in the pond!

But for most of the animals, the thunderstorm was noisy and frightening. Even old Owl tried to cover his head with his wings and hide from the rumbling roars.

Slowly the storm clouds moved over the woods, and the lightning and thunder stopped. As the dark clouds passed, the sky turned pink and gold. The storm was over, and the birds began to sing again.

In his quiet thicket Bambi fell asleep at last, and his dreams were filled with his new friends and their adventures.

CHAPTER THREE

As spring turned into summer, Bambi learned how to do more and more things. He could now easily keep up with his mother on their daily walks. Together they explored the woods, and he learned to find places where there was food to eat and water to drink. As he discovered new things about the world, Bambi had new questions to ask.

Early one morning the curious fawn wondered, "Mother, what are we going to do today?"

"I'm going to take you to the meadow," said his mother.

"What's the meadow?" Bambi asked, running with her.

"It's a very wonderful place," she told him.

"Then why haven't we been there before?" he asked.

"You weren't big enough," she said. Bambi's mother looked at her young fawn. He was getting stronger every day. His long legs were no longer wobbly, and he walked with confidence past the waterfall.

"Mother, you know what?" he asked.

"What?" said his mother.

"Thumper told me we're not the only deer in the forest," Bambi said.

"Well, he's right," she said. "There are many deer in the forest besides us."

"Then why don't I ever see them?" Bambi asked.

"You will, sometime," his mother said.

"On the meadow?" the curious fawn asked.

"Perhaps," said his mother. "Hush, now."

His mother stopped and carefully looked all around. She turned her long ears this way and that and listened for any sign of danger.

"We're almost there," she whispered to Bambi.

At the edge of the woods, the clusters of tall trees ended. Ahead of Bambi was a wide, empty place, filled with sunlight and flowers. It looked beautiful, and Bambi could not wait to get there.

"The meadow!" he cried, dashing ahead of his mother into the lovely fields. Without any trees or bushes to stop him, Bambi could run in any direction he wished. He could run as free through the meadow as a bird could fly in the open sky.

"Bambi, wait!" called his mother. She leapt in front of him, blocking his way. "You must *never* rush out on the meadow," she said firmly.

Bambi heard the fear in her voice, and he became frightened.

"There might be danger," she explained. "Out there we are unprotected."

Bambi looked around at the emptiness of the meadow. He looked at the green sloping fields and the bright sky above.

"The meadow is wide and open, and there are no trees or bushes to hide us," his mother continued. "So we have to be very careful."

This was a new lesson for Bambi, and he listened to his mother, ready to obey her.

"Wait here," she said. "I'll go out first, and if the meadow's safe, I'll call you."

Bambi tucked himself into the grass so no one could find him. He had learned well how to hide.

As he watched, his mother stepped carefully onto the meadow, looking this way and that way. She moved slowly, stopping to listen for any noise that might reveal danger. It was hard for her to see clearly in the early morning mist, and as she moved away from Bambi she seemed to fade in the mist, too. But Bambi waited patiently and listened for her call.

The doe's ears turned as she picked up the soft sound of birds chirping as they flew above her. A flock of small birds landed and disappeared in the grass ahead. Their calls told her they did not see any danger. The meadow was safe for now.

"Come on, Bambi," she said. "It's all right."

Bambi crept cautiously from his hiding place. Then he ran to his mother, who was waiting for him.

They ran together through the grass, leaping in one direction and then another, whichever way they wished. It was delightful to run in the meadow. Bambi skipped through the grass that tickled his legs, and he leapt over the colorful flowers. Above him there were no trees to hide the bright blue sky and drifting clouds.

Bambi discovered a tiny brook where ducklings were learning to swim. He leapt happily over the brook. Then he bounded into the shallow waters, splashing himself and the ducklings, too. This was fun!

Other animals from the woods were visiting the meadow that day, too. Bambi discovered the rabbit family as they were eating their breakfast. "Good morning, Prince Bambi," the rabbits called.

"Hello," said Bambi, watching them curiously. "What are you eating?"

"Clover," the rabbits said. "It's awfully good!"

"It's delicious," mumbled Thumper, hidden under a big batch of green leaves and purple flowers. "Why don't you try some?"

Bambi grabbed a big mouthful of leaves.

"No, no," cried Thumper, "not that green stuff."

Sitting among the purple flowers, Thumper leaned over, opened his mouth, and started to eat one of them.

"Thumper!" scolded his mother. The little rabbit stopped eating the flower and looked at her.

30

"Yes, Mama," he said.

"What did your father tell you?" she asked him.

Thumper paused and asked, "About what, Mama?" His father had a great deal to say about a great many different things.

"What did your father say about eating the blossoms and leaving the greens?" his mother asked him.

"Oh, that one!" said Thumper.

He recited from memory his father's lesson: "Eating greens is a special treat. It makes long ears and great big feet." Thumper patted his long ear and raised his big foot to show them as proof of his father's lesson.

Then he whispered into Bambi's ear, "But it sure is awful stuff to eat!" No one except Bambi heard him, and Thumper added proudly, "I made that last part up myself!"

CHAPTER FOUR

Hearing Thumper talk so much about flowers made Bambi want to try one, too. But when he reached for a purple blossom, a frog, hiding underneath the flower, jumped out and surprised him. Bambi decided it would be more fun to chase the frog than to eat.

"Watch out! Watch out!" croaked the frog, leaping from place to place. With a loud splash, he disappeared into the pond.

Bambi looked at the spot in the water where the frog had vanished. But instead of a frog, he saw a fawn. Who was this fawn looking at him? he wondered. Bambi bent over to sniff the young fawn in the pond. His nose touched the cold water, and Bambi pulled his wet face back in surprise. He had never seen his own reflection before.

The surface of the pond rippled in circles. When the pond was calm again, Bambi looked down. Now he saw the faces of not one fawn, but two! How could that be?

One of the fawns smiled and giggled. Bambi looked up and saw her standing on the other side of the water. She was watching him.

Bambi was so startled that he didn't know what to do. He backed

away, but the strange fawn followed him. He tripped over some roots and fell, and then he ran and ran quickly away from the pond. But the fawn ran fast, too, and she chased him through the grass.

Bambi dashed to his mother at the top of the hill. She was eating the grass there, and she was not alone. Another doe was with her.

Bambi tried to hide under his mother's tall legs. She looked at both her frightened son and the little fawn chasing him. "That's little Faline," Bambi's mother said.

Faline watched Bambi, wagging her tail in friendship.

"He's bashful, isn't he, Mama?" Faline asked her mother.

"Maybe he wouldn't be if you'd say hello," suggested her mother.

Faline leapt toward Bambi and stared right at him.

"Hello, Bambi," she said.

But Bambi still wasn't sure of her. He had met all sorts of animals, but he had never been this close to another fawn before.

Faline couldn't understand why Bambi didn't answer her.

"I said hello!" the fawn repeated.

"Well," said Bambi's mother, trying to help him out. "Aren't you going to answer her? You're not afraid, are you?"

Bambi knew he wasn't afraid. No, that wasn't it. He was just shy.

"Well then, go ahead," said his mother, nudging him toward Faline. "Go on, Bambi, say hello!" she said.

Very embarrassed, Bambi whispered, "Hello."

His shyness made Faline giggle again. She ran toward Bambi and playfully chased him. He started to back up into some rushes, but he landed instead in a puddle of water. While Bambi sat there, Faline peeked through the tall rushes, playing a game of hide-and-seek.

She dashed from one side to the other, licking his face when he wasn't looking. Faline was having fun teasing him, but Bambi was getting annoyed.

"Yeeowww!" he shouted finally. The young prince jumped up and began to chase Faline. He knew what to do now! Faline ran and hid under her mother's legs, giggling as Bambi charged toward her.

The two does watched as the fawns played and ran after each other across the meadow. Faline bounded on top of a big rock in the middle of the field and looked to see if Bambi was coming. He leapt from a different direction and surprised her by landing on the rock, too. Out of breath, they both giggled, enjoying a new good game together.

But the two fawns were not alone in the middle of the meadow. They heard the sound of hooves pounding on the earth. The fawns

turned and saw a herd of deer—large male stags with sharp antlers on their heads—coming their way.

The stags bounded across the field, leaping far and high as they ran. As the two fawns watched, two males stopped and turned to each other, locking horns to test their strength.

Bambi tried to imitate the stags. He rushed at Faline, butting his soft head against hers, but this was not a game she wanted to play. So she ran off to play by herself.

Curious about the stags, Bambi stayed behind to watch them as they bounded up the rocks and jumped off the tallest one. He tried to follow and run up the tall rocks, too. But he was not big enough or strong enough to leap as far as they could.

Bambi had never seen such graceful and powerful animals. He wished he could race as swiftly as they could.

Fascinated, Bambi followed the herd until the stags stopped abruptly. Bambi ran among them and turned to see what had caught their attention. What were they looking at? he wondered.

A great stag stood at the edge of the forest. He was taller than any of the others, and his many-branched antlers were the largest of all.

Bambi saw the great stag walk regally from the woods into the clearing. The fawn had seen so many new things today, but he had never seen such a grand and majestic creature before.

As the stag walked past Bambi, he stopped and gazed down at the tiny fawn before moving on.

Bambi could not believe that the stag had noticed him.

"He stopped and looked at me," Bambi told his mother as she came up beside him.

"Yes, I know," said his mother. She smiled proudly at her fawn.

"Why was everyone still when he came on the meadow?" Bambi asked.

"Everyone respects him," said Bambi's mother. "Of all the deer in the forest, not one has lived half so long."

Bambi's eyes followed the stag as he entered the forest again and climbed a wooded hill.

"He's very brave and very wise," Bambi's mother said. "That's why he's known as the Great Prince of the Forest."

In the woods the great stag listened and heard birds cawing as they flew in panic over his head. He could hear and see their fright.

There was danger coming! He raced down the hill to the meadow. All the deer stopped eating and playing when they saw him burst from the forest. They sensed he was coming to warn them of danger.

All the animals in the meadow raced through the empty fields to the woods, where they would be safe.

Faline's mother rushed through the panicked animals, looking for her daughter. When she found her, the two deer ran to their home in the forest.

But Bambi's mother did not see her fawn. She looked for him and dashed back and forth, calling, "Bambi! Bambi!"

Bambi sensed the danger everywhere and looked for his mother, too. "Mother!" he called, hoping she would hear him and come find him. He had never been as frightened before. He could not see her or hear her or catch her scent. Where was she?

Suddenly a large stag stood over Bambi. It was his father, the Great Prince, who was looking down at him. Bambi followed the stag, and his mother saw them and joined them. Together the three deer ran from the danger, which was coming closer and closer.

Bam! Bam! The loud noise of gunfire rocked the woods. Birds screamed, and then there was just silence.

In the forest Bambi's mother stood very still and listened. She waited until she was sure that the hunters had passed. Then she turned to the place where her fawn was hidden.

"Come on out, Bambi," she said. "It's safe now. We don't have to hide any longer."

Bambi obeyed and joined her. "What happened, Mother?" the curious fawn asked. "Why did we all run?"

Bambi's mother looked at her son and paused, trying to find the way to help him understand this greatest of all dangers. How could she explain hunters to a tiny fawn? So she simply named the danger.

"Man was in the forest," she said.

Quietly Bambi's mother led her fawn home, very glad that the hunters were gone this day.

C H A P T E R   F I V E

As summer turned to fall, Bambi saw his world changing more and more every day. The grasses in the meadow grew tall and turned brown. Throughout the forest, the leaves on the trees, once bright green, turned red and gold and orange. Bambi looked at the tall trees decorated in brilliant fall colors.

Unlike the warm days of summer, fall days were cool and the nights chilly. Many animals were leaving the forest and moving to warmer places. Each day, Bambi watched another flock of birds leave their homes in the woods and fly south.

But Bambi and the other deer stayed behind. They looked together for fallen acorns and nuts to eat and watched as the leaves began to fall from the trees. The delicate leaves drifted and swirled in the cool winds and landed everywhere. Wherever Bambi walked in the woods, bright colorful leaves covered the ground. As he walked by the stream, leaves danced down around him, landing and floating on the water. Why were the leaves falling? he wondered.

Looking up, Bambi could now see sky peeking through the once-bushy treetops. Each day, he saw more bare trees and bushes. Even

his thicket had changed. All the tiny leaves from the bushes had fallen to the ground. Bare twigs surrounded him and his mother as they slept. In the fall, Bambi learned, trees lose their leaves, birds fly away, and life starts to change in the woods.

One morning Bambi woke up early. It was unusually bright outside his thicket. The light made him blink and blink. He crept out and looked at the woods. His world had changed again!

Where were the bare trees? Bambi wondered. Where was the dark ground covered with leaves? Everything was hidden in a coat of white. He couldn't stop blinking at the bright white world all around him.

"Mother, look!" he cried excitedly. "What's all that white stuff?"

Waking up, his mother looked out, too. "Why, it's snow," she said gently, remembering fondly her first glimpse of snow.

"Snow?" asked Bambi.

"Yes," explained his mother. "Winter has come."

Bambi sniffed the snow and tested it with one hoof. He sank into the soft snow, and when he pulled his hoof out, it left a hole. This was certainly amazing, he thought.

He walked through the snow, looking back at his own footprints. It was fun to step and make more and more prints in the snow. Bambi was so busy making footprints, he didn't look where he was going. *Whoosh!* Bambi sank into a big hole that had been covered by the snow. The cold, wet snow tickled him and chilled him.

Brrr! Snow was tricky and full of surprises, too, he thought.

Bambi was too curious to let a little cold snow frighten him. He got up and began exploring the snowy woods.

All around him Bambi heard the bell-like sounds of icicles touching and the soft, whooshing sounds of snow falling from the trees. He looked up at the snow that covered the branches above him. *Plop! Plop!* Some of that snow was falling very close to him. Bambi leapt away.

It seemed as if the snow were playing a game with Bambi, trying to catch him and get him wet. He tried to outguess the snow and stay dry . . . but it wasn't easy.

Whoosh! Plop!

A chunk of soft snow landed right on top of Bambi. *Brrrrr!* He shook and shook himself free. This was a funny game that winter was playing today.

Bambi wasn't the only young animal playing in snow for the first time. Thumper had discovered snow, too, and he was having lots of fun.

"Look, Bambi," Thumper called. "Watch what I can do."

The lively rabbit ran and ran down a snowbank. He leapt into the air and slid on his furry bottom across the icy pond.

"Wheee!" the rabbit called. The frozen pond was smooth and hard, and Thumper glided across the icy surface. This was fun!

Amazed, Bambi watched his friend. How could Thumper do that? he wondered. What had happened to the pond?

Thumper grinned at Bambi. "Come on, it's all right," he tried to explain. "Look," said the rabbit, thumping his foot on the hard ice. "The water's stiff!"

Bambi couldn't wait to try sliding and skating on the pond, too, and he ran down a snowy slope as fast as he could. He leapt into

the air, just as Thumper had done. "Yippee," he called, and he landed on the ice. But his legs were very long and his hooves very small. They slipped out from under him, and he fell on the ice, spinning and spinning on his tummy. Skating looked different when Thumper did it.

Thumper skated up to his friend and said, "Some fun, huh, Bambi?" Bambi nodded yes, but he wasn't sure yet.

"Come on, get up," said Thumper. "Like this." The little rabbit ran on the ice and skated all around on his big flat feet. Bambi could see it was easy to skate—if you had the right feet.

The young fawn tried to get up, but it was a lot harder to walk on the ice than on the ground. His hooves slipped out from under him, and he fell again.

"No, no, no," cried Thumper, laughing. The little rabbit tried

to help his friend get up. He pushed and pulled and tugged at Bambi's legs.

"A little wobbly, aren't you," said Thumper, but he didn't stop trying to help.

Finally Bambi stood up, and Thumper gave him a big push. The fawn started to glide and glide. But his hind legs twisted underneath him, and he sat down hard on the ice.

"You have to watch both ends at the same time," Thumper said, looking at Bambi's front and hind legs. Thumper helped him unwind his legs and get up, and then he gave Bambi another big push.

Wheeee! Bambi slid across the ice fast—very fast. It was a little scary for him to move so swiftly. But Thumper ran in front of him, cheering him on. When Bambi slipped, he and Thumper sailed along the pond together.

"Wow!" cried Thumper, enjoying the ride.

But Bambi didn't know how to stop, so they crashed into a soft snowbank. The two friends weren't hurt at all, but they *were* very wet.

Thumper quickly popped up and shook the snow from his long ears. He heard something, and the curious rabbit hopped up to the opening of a small den. Someone inside was snoring very loudly.

It was Flower. The tiny skunk was fast asleep.

The curious rabbit grinned and began thumping very loudly. "Wake up! Wake up!" Thumper called.

"Wake up, Flower," called Bambi, smiling, too.

The sleeping skunk heard his friends and opened his eyes.

"Is it spring yet?" Flower asked them drowsily.

"No," said Bambi. "Winter is just starting."

"What are you doing? Hibernating?" Thumper asked.

"Uh-huh," said Flower, rubbing his tired eyes and scratching his furry legs.

"Why do you want to do that?" asked Bambi. He couldn't imagine anyone sleeping when there was snow to enjoy everywhere.

The little skunk giggled shyly. "Hee! Hee! All us flowers sleep in the winter. Hee! Hee!"

It was very hard for a very sleepy skunk to stay awake even to talk with his friends. Soon Flower curled up and wrapped his long, warm tail around himself.

"Well," he said, closing his eyes, "good night."

Then he fell asleep once more, and his two friends left him to dream and rest until spring. Together Bambi and Thumper went off to play their new winter games.

CHAPTER SIX

Bambi soon learned that winter days were not always such happy ones. The brown, dead grass in the meadow was buried under drifts of snow, and there were no tangy leaves on the bushes. The deer spent their days hunting for food, and what they found to eat was never enough.

Winter was a hard time for all the animals who remained in the woods and stayed awake all season long. In some ways, the animals, like Flower, who slept through the long winter were more fortunate than those who did not hibernate.

Some winters, like this one, were very harsh. Even in his warm furry coat, Bambi could feel the frigid winds. He shivered, following his mother through the blinding snowstorms. They could not hide in their thicket from the snow. They had to stay outside and search for food.

The deer began to eat the bark on the young trees. At first they stripped off pieces of bark near the ground. As they failed to find other food, the deer stripped the bark higher and higher up the tree trunks.

While snow blew around her, Bambi's mother reached high, standing against a tree, to get a strip of bark. She gave it to her fawn, and he gobbled it up quickly.

Bambi and his mother wandered through the woods day after day, hoping to find something to eat that others had missed. But one day all the young trees were stripped of bark as high as Bambi's mother could reach. She licked her fawn's face tenderly. If only there were some food she could give him.

The two hungry deer went home without supper.

"Winter sure is long, isn't it?" Bambi asked.

"It seems long, but it won't last forever," his mother said, hoping to comfort him.

As they rested, Bambi snuggled against her and tried to stay warm.

"I'm awfully hungry, Mother," he told her.

"Yes, I know," she said, touching him gently till he fell asleep. For her young fawn's sake, she wished with all her heart that winter would end soon.

One morning Bambi's mother took him to the snow-covered meadow. She noticed a difference in the air. It was a little warmer, and tiny streams had begun to thaw and trickle through the field.

"Look," she called to Bambi. There was a green patch in the snow.

"It's new spring grass," she said, and the two deer ran to it. Bambi gobbled the grass. Nothing had ever tasted so good to him, and he wished he could keep on eating until he was full.

Suddenly his mother stopped eating. She stretched her long neck

and looked all around her. She sniffed the air and turned her long ears to hear a soft crunching in the snow. Someone was nearby!

"Bambi!" she called, frightened. "Quick! Go to the thicket!"

Bambi obeyed and ran across the snowy field. He leapt over the tiny melting streams. His mother followed him quickly.

"Faster," she called to him. "Faster, Bambi."

He heard the fear in her voice, and he looked back to catch sight of her.

"Don't look back!" she called firmly. "Keep running!"

Bambi ran across the snowy meadow and into the forest. Behind him a loud noise blasted. *Bam!* He ran faster, not looking back, remembering his mother's words. The young deer kept on running through the woods until he reached his home.

"We made it!" he called, stopping to take a breath at last. He waited, but he did not hear his mother's footsteps. Where was she?

"Mother," he called, and ran outside.

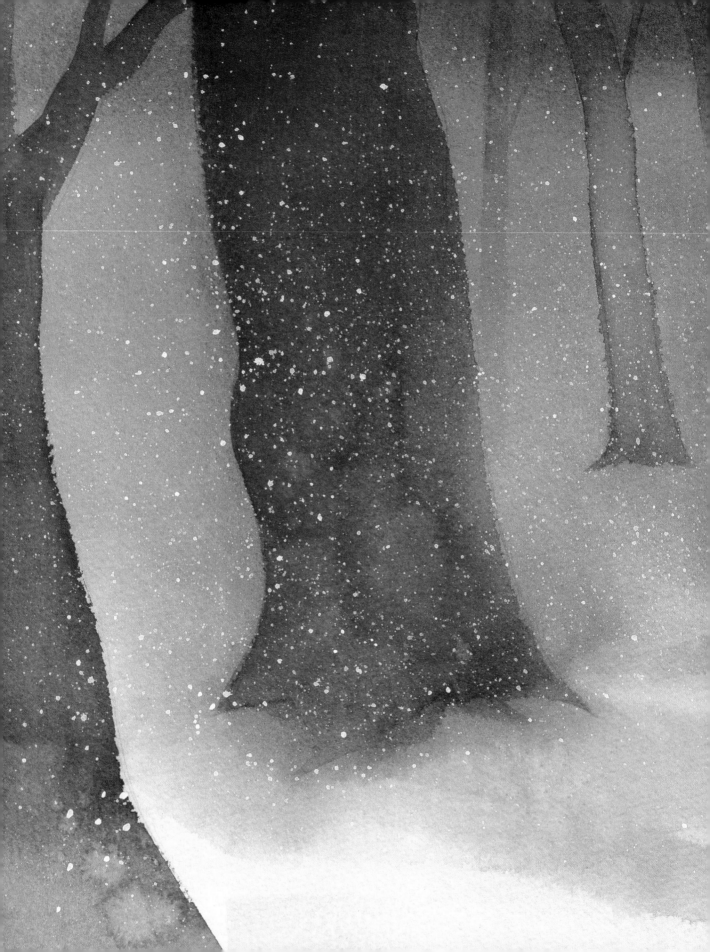

All around him, snow was falling. He hoped to see his mother running toward him. But he did not, and he began to cry.

"Mother," Bambi called again, and he wandered through the storm looking for her. It was so hard to see anything or anyone through the curtain of falling snow.

Suddenly a shadowy shape appeared, and Bambi jumped back. He looked hard through the blinding snow and saw the figure of the Great Prince in front of him.

"Your mother," said the stag in a deep, sad voice, "can't be with you anymore."

Stunned, Bambi remembered his mother's fear and the loud noise. He remembered that noise as part of the danger his mother had called "man" long ago. Hunters had come to the forest again, and this time they had taken his mother away.

As Bambi cried softly, thinking of her, the large stag spoke gently. "Come, my son." The stag knew it was time for him to watch over Bambi and keep him safe.

Bambi followed his father through the woods. But he stopped now and then to look back, missing his mother. He would never forget her, and he would always remember her love for him.

CHAPTER SEVEN

Bambi's first winter was harsh and sad. But no winter lasts forever. When spring finally came, all the animals were ready to celebrate a new season of life and joy.

In the warm springtime the forest was reborn. Tiny new green leaves danced on all the trees. Dainty flowers of every color dotted the ground below.

In each tree and on every branch there seemed to be birds singing louder and sweeter than anyone could remember. The birds had returned from their winter homes and were busy looking for mates. They flew through the trees, chasing each other in wild, wonderful dances, all the while singing their merry spring songs.

All this noise woke up poor Owl in his tree.

"Ohhhh, what now," sleepy Owl muttered. "Hey, stop that racket."

He looked at the cheerful, romantic birds with disgust. All this billing and cooing was just too much for him.

"Scat!" Owl cried, flapping his wings to chase the birds away. "Shoo! Shoo!"

But the happy birds didn't pay him any attention. They sang as loud as before.

"I'll fix them," Owl mumbled. He made an angry face and cried as loud as he could, "Woo! Woo!"

The scared birds flew away quickly. Owl listened, and the woods around him were quiet once more.

"There! I guess that will teach them," he said smugly.

Yet before he could blink twice, the birds were back and singing again!

"Ohhh, what's the use," Owl moaned, and he flew off to find a quieter tree. He found a good spot and settled down.

"Same thing every spring. '*Tweet! Tweet! Tweet!*'" Owl said, mimicking the singing birds. "Love's sweet song! Pain in the pin-feathers, I'd call it!"

He was just settling down to a nice nap when the tree began to tremble and shake. Owl had to hang on for dear life.

"Stop it!" he shouted. He looked down, and his blurry eyes seemed to see a whole bunch of animals shaking his tree.

"Get out of here—all of you," said Owl.

But it wasn't a bunch of animals. It was just one male deer rubbing his antlers against the trunk. His antlers were new and itchy. Scratching them against the rough bark made the deer feel better.

When he heard Owl, the stag stopped and looked up.

"Hello, friend Owl," he said. "Don't you remember me?"

"Why, it's the young prince!" Owl said. "My, my, how you've changed. Turn around there, Bambi, and let me look at you."

Bambi turned so Owl could see how much taller he was and how much he had changed.

"I see you've traded in your spots for a pair of antlers," Owl said.

Bambi tossed his head, proud of his fine antlers. Owl chuckled, pleased to see how Bambi had grown into such a fine young stag.

"You know, just the other day, I was talking to myself about you," Owl said, "and we were wondering what had become of you."

Just then another voice called out, "Hello, Bambi!"

The voice sounded like Thumper's, but it was deeper. The rabbit that hopped toward Bambi was larger, too. But this large rabbit was Bambi's same bold and lively old friend.

"Remember me?" said the rabbit, thumping on the ground with his big foot.

"Thumper!" called Bambi.

"Righto," said the rabbit.

A black-and-white head popped up from a patch of daisies.

"Hi, fellows," said a big skunk. He was awake now from his long winter's nap.

"Flower!" called Bambi.

"Yeah," said Flower, sniffing the new daisies all around him.

The three friends were happy to be together again. They had all grown bigger and stronger, but they still felt the same about each other.

A pair of birds flew over their heads, dancing in midair and acting rather silly, or so the friends thought.

"Well, what's the matter with them?" Flower wondered.

"Why are they acting that way?" Thumper asked Owl.

Owl laughed at their confusion. "Why, don't you know?" he said. "They're *twitterpated*!"

"Twitterpated?" cried the three friends. What was that? they wondered. It sounded terrible.

"Nearly everybody gets twitterpated in the springtime," Owl tried to explain. "For example, you're walking along, minding your

own business. Then, all of a sudden, you run right smack into a pretty face!"

Owl cringed and tried to hide. "Woo! Woo!" he called, and flapped his wings, frightening his listeners even more.

"You begin to get weak in the knees," he said, "and then you feel light as a feather. And before you know it, you're walking on air."

He glided high into the air as they watched, amazed.

"And then you know what! You're knocked for a loop," he said, spinning around a branch. "You completely lose your head."

Owl tucked his head inside his feathers till it disappeared. He looked headless!

"Gosh!" said Thumper, horrified. "That's awful."

Owl enjoyed being dramatic, and he saw he had his audience's full attention now.

"And it can happen to anybody! So you better be careful," he warned them, creeping closer and closer.

"It could happen to you!" he cried, pointing to Bambi.

"And you!" he cried, pointing to Thumper.

"Yes, it could even happen to you!" he cried, pointing to Flower.

The three animals were stunned. They could become twitterpated! What a horrible thought!

"Well, it's not going to happen to me," said Thumper firmly.

"Me, neither," promised Bambi and Flower together.

The three friends looked at each other and nodded in agreement. No matter what Owl thought, *they* were never going to be twitterpated. They marched away, confident that would never happen to them.

As they walked through the forest, other animals watched them pass. A young female skunk noticed Flower. He looked like such a nice skunk, she wished he would notice her. She was shy, too, and hid in some flowers. As Flower passed by, she giggled.

The flowers shook all around her, and Flower caught a glimpse of her. He moved a little closer. Who was hiding there? he wondered. Someone was being very mysterious.

Flower crept closer and closer until he could see it was a little skunk, just like him. The two shy animals looked at each other. Softly their noses touched, and Flower felt different. He tumbled backward in delight.

Down the path, Bambi and Thumper slowly realized that Flower was no longer following them. When they turned to look for him, they saw two striped tails rising from the field of flowers. Their friend popped up from the flowers, shrugged, and giggled happily.

Thumper watched the two skunks head off together and shook his head. "Twitterpated," he said.

Bambi and Thumper stuck together as they walked through the woods. But before long, a young female rabbit saw Thumper. She made a soft sound that caught his attention. She hummed to him, and he watched her and listened to her. She certainly did not look like any rabbit he had seen before. She was so soft and furry. Her ears were so long and dainty.

She hopped closer to him and whispered, "Hello."

Startled, Thumper didn't know how to react. His foot started thumping out of control. *Thump, thump, thump.* The young female rabbit saw how nervous he was, and she touched him gently to calm him. He stopped thumping and simply stared at this kind, gentle rabbit. How wonderful she seemed! he thought. How beautiful, how sweet!

When Bambi stopped hearing Thumper's footsteps behind him, he turned around and saw two rabbits playing together. One was thumping with joy. Both were very twitterpated.

Oh no, thought Bambi, shaking his head. Not Thumper, too. Now he was the only sensible one left.

Bambi continued on his way, enjoying the lovely spring day and the woods all around him. He walked into a shallow pool of water that was no longer frozen and took a drink. As he did he saw the reflection of another deer in the water. This deer had no antlers on her head.

He heard a voice say, "Hello, Bambi!"

When he looked up, he was startled to see a doe looking at him.

"Don't you remember me?" she said. "I'm Faline."

She moved toward Bambi in a friendly way, but he backed up, not knowing what to do or say. She had caught him by surprise, just as she had long ago. Suddenly he tripped and sat down in the water.

Embarrassed, Bambi retreated, but Faline followed him. Bambi was so nervous he backed into a branch full of flowers. His new antlers caught on the branch and got tangled in it. Bambi felt very foolish and awkward. But Faline simply came close and licked his face softly, as she had done when they were younger. This time it felt different to Bambi. It felt nice, very nice.

At that moment Bambi was both slightly confused and completely happy. He remembered what Owl had said. "You begin to get weak in the knees, and then you feel light as a feather. And before you know it, you're walking on air."

That's how I feel, Bambi thought. I must be twitterpated. But it didn't matter anymore. All he could think of was Faline.

Bambi leapt gaily after her across the meadow where they had played as fawns. He felt as if he could jump higher than any stag and even soar over the clouds. He followed Faline, feeling as if they were floating together in a wonderful dream.

But their dream ended abruptly when a stag sprang from the bushes and stood between Bambi and Faline. The stag lowered his head and jerked his antlers threateningly until Bambi backed away from the sharp points.

Bambi stared over the stag at Faline. She was just as surprised. He tried to go around the stranger, and Faline tried to do the same.

The stag thrust himself between them again. Contemptuously he

turned his back on Bambi. Bowing his head, he tossed his antlers at Faline.

"Bambi!" she called.

With quick bobs of his head, the stag drove Faline deeper into the woods, away from Bambi.

Bambi heard Faline's cries, and he pawed the ground in anger. He lowered his head and charged at the stag. With a powerful spring, the stag darted toward Bambi. They raced toward each other, but at the last moment the stag shifted to one side, catching Bambi's body on his antlers. With a toss of his head, he threw Bambi to the ground.

Bambi rose, stunned and dazed. Just in time he turned his head and saw the stag charging again. Bambi had never fought this way

before. He felt the shock as their antlers clashed and locked together. With a quick, powerful twist of his head, the stag threw Bambi down into the dirt.

Again and again the two stags charged at each other. They rammed each other with their antlers and pushed and shoved each other to the ground. The other stag was more experienced, but Bambi was quickly learning how to fight.

Lowering his head, Bambi aimed his antlers at his enemy and charged. The ground raced by before his eyes. His hooves pounded rhythmically. This time he was ready for the shock of the impact.

With a loud clatter, he locked horns with the stag. While the stag was off balance, Bambi shifted his hooves. The stag swung through the air. With a quick dip of his shoulders, Bambi threw him hard against the ground.

The stag rolled over and over through the dirt and the weeds and down a steep slope straight into the stream. Bambi waited on the bank for the stag to attack again. But the stranger rose dejectedly in the water and floundered away.

Bambi had won.

Faline, who had watched the fight in fear, rushed to Bambi's side. She brushed her face against him, glad he wasn't hurt. He brushed his face against hers, glad she was safe.

Together they walked through the forest as if they were seeing it for the first time. Then they ran through the meadow as day turned to night. They ran, not chasing each other now, but as partners— a pair of deer sharing their world. In the evening, wind blew through the grass and fireflies lit the way of two deer who had found each other. For them this spring day had marked the beginning of a lasting bond.

CHAPTER EIGHT

Bambi and Faline enjoyed the lush spring and summer days together. When the leaves began to change color and drift from the trees, they knew that fall was coming again.

Early one fall morning, something woke Bambi. He stood up, careful not to wake Faline, who was sleeping beside him. A strange scent drifted through the woods, and cautiously Bambi searched for it. The scent led him up a cliff where, in the distance, he could see a tall column of smoke rising from campfires below.

Silently his father joined him on the cliff. The older stag said, "It's man. He is here again."

The two stags stared at the danger that was nearby once more. They could hear the cawing of birds who, at first, circled above the camp and then began to flee toward the woods.

"There are many men this time," said the great stag. "We must go deep into the forest—hurry!"

The stag leapt through the brush, away from the cliff. Bambi began to follow until he remembered Faline. He had to warn her, and they had to find a safe place in the woods together.

He ran toward their resting place. But the crying calls of the birds had disturbed Faline's sleep. She awoke, wondered what was wrong, and turned toward Bambi. He was not at her side.

"Bambi!" Faline called. She knew he wouldn't leave her in danger. Perhaps something had happened to him. She could not see or hear him nearby. Frightened for him, she bolted into the woods, calling, "Bambi!"

When Bambi returned, she was gone. "Faline!" he called, fearful for her. In his panic he could not tell which path she had taken. He ran off, but he took a different path in the woods.

"*Caw! Caw!*" Birds screamed overhead, relaying a message of fear to all the animals in the forest and meadow.

Everyone rushed for safety. Thumper and his mate gathered their children, and they hopped quickly away, trying to stay out of the hunters' sight.

Animals hid in trees and in holes in the ground—in any place

that seemed to be safe from the heavy tread of the hunters moving closer and closer.

The tall meadow grasses provided hiding places for pheasants who listened and waited for a hunter to pass.

"Listen," whispered a frightened pheasant. "He's coming!"

"Hush," another bird tried to calm her.

"Be quiet," said a third.

"He's coming closer!" said the first pheasant. "We better fly!"

"No, no," whispered another. "Don't fly—whatever you do, don't fly!"

But in her fright the pheasant wasn't listening to anything but the sound of heavy footsteps too close to bear.

"He's almost here!" she said, fluttering her wings and running along the ground. "I can't stand it any longer!"

And the frightened bird flew into the air, where the hunters could see her.

Bam! Bam! Shotguns roared, and the pheasant fell lifelessly to the ground.

Again and again the guns roared as terrified animals ran through the meadow and the woods. They had to run out of reach of the hunters' terrible weapons. They had to find safe places to hide.

The hunters had dogs to help them find their prey. A pack of excited dogs ran toward Faline and chased her. The lead dog nipped at her heels. The pack ran barking and howling, their mouths open and filled with sharp teeth.

Faline ran in panic through the woods, but the dogs outnumbered her. She bounded up a rocky hill and stood on a narrow ledge while the dogs leapt up, trying to reach her.

"Bambi!" she shouted.

In the distance Bambi heard her cries and the sounds of the angry dogs. He ran through the woods faster than he ever had before. He saw Faline shaking in fear just above the pack of snarling dogs.

Furious, Bambi lowered his head and rammed into the dogs, tossing them right and left with his antlers. They climbed on his back and nipped at him. He tossed them off one by one. Dogs bit his long legs, and he kicked them with his strong hooves. But there were so many dogs and just one deer to fight them all. Bambi might not be able to beat them, but he would at least distract them from Faline.

"Quick, Faline," he called to her. "Jump!"

While the dogs were busy fighting Bambi, Faline leapt from her ledge and escaped up another rocky slope.

Bambi let the pack of dogs surround and attack him until he knew Faline was safely away. Then he fought his way free and headed after her, the angry dogs following at his heels.

As Bambi ran up the slope, sharp rocks slipped under his hooves and poured down on the dogs behind him. The dogs, pelted by the falling rocks, fell backward.

The powerful young stag raced onward through the forest. At the edge of a deep ravine Bambi leapt toward the other side. It seemed he was safely across when . . .

Bam!

Bambi crumpled to the ground. He had crossed the ravine, but he had been shot. The injured stag raised his head and tried to get up, but he could not.

Bambi lay on the ground, too weak to stand. In his pain he thought of Faline. At least she was safe.

CHAPTER NINE

As day ended and it grew too dark to see and hunt, the hunters returned to their camp. Before they went to sleep in their tents, no one checked the campfire to see if it was put out. While the hunters slept, the fall wind blew through the campground. The wind scattered leaves on the ground, and sparks from the campfire, still smoldering and alive, flared. Leaves and grass caught fire, and the bright flames lit up the night.

Aided by the wind, fire spread quickly through the dry brown grasses and up the tree trunks into the branches. Birds flew from their nests, and small animals ran from their homes, which were now in flames.

Smoke made a foul-smelling haze in the forest. Bambi lifted his head as the scent of smoke pricked at his nostrils. He took a deep breath, and the smoke filled his lungs. Still weak and hurt, he sensed the danger in the forest.

He heard a voice command him, "Get up, Bambi!"

Bambi saw his father standing over him, watching him with care and concern. "Get up!" his father shouted.

Bambi tried to move, but pain shot through his body. He fell back to the ground.

"You *must* get up!" said his father, who could see the fire coming closer and closer to his son.

Bambi tried to obey, but it was too painful to stand.

Bambi's father could see the flames leap to a nearby tree. He could hardly breathe as smoke filled the air around them. He knew that his son could not stay here any longer. "Get up," he repeated. "Get up."

Once again Bambi tried to stand, and this time he succeeded. He was hurt, but he could move—he *would* move.

His father stood beside him and said, "Now, come with me!"

The great stag led his son through the treacherous woods. As the wind changed its course, fire darted in different directions. At first the flames were behind them, but then they blocked the deer's path.

The great stag used all his wisdom and experience to fight the wind and the fire to find the safest path through the forest. He knew that Bambi was too tired to find his way alone, so he guided his son, making sure he stayed close. And as he ran, Bambi felt stronger knowing that his father was with him. Together they would make it safely through the burning woods.

The stags leapt into a stream, hoping that the water would protect them from the blaze. They ran along the streambed, but the wind shifted again. Suddenly the fire was in front of them. They turned around and ran back, but trees along the banks of the stream were ablaze, too. Burning limbs fell into the water, one almost brushing against Bambi.

They ran until the stream in front of them cascaded down as a waterfall. The stags could not safely go any farther. But behind them a tall tree, its trunk burning wildly, started to fall on top of

them. They had no retreat. They had to leap over the waterfall.

With great courage, the two deer jumped down and down and crashed into the water far below.

At the edge of the forest was a broad lake. Many animals had found safety on an island in the lake. Birds flew and rested in the trees there. Their tiny bodies lined the branches as they slept.

Mother Opossum carried her babies on her tail as she swam to safety. And raccoons gently carried their young in their mouths to the island, too.

Nearby, Faline stood, looking back at the forest, at the hills, and at the sky behind them red with flames. She watched the other animals group together, and she felt so alone.

Exhausted, the young doe could not rest. She stared at the lake

and the forest, waiting. As she listened she heard the soft splashing sound of someone moving through the water.

Through the smoky haze she saw two figures walking slowly in the shallow water. They looked very tired. She recognized their strong bodies, their broad antlers.

"Bambi!" she called.

Bambi dashed through the water toward Faline's voice. He climbed up on the rock beside her. She was alive! The fire had almost cost him his life, but they had both survived.

Grateful to be safe, the two deer stayed close, waiting for the fire to die out so they could return to their woods together.

C H A P T E R   T E N

The fire burned much of the forest and left many of the animals homeless. But a forest can survive a fire. By spring, new green seedlings were shooting up near the scorched tree trunks. In time they would be young, tall trees. Through the ashes, new shoots sprouted, and from them, flowers would soon bloom. Life was going on.

Where the woods were spared, the animals made new homes for themselves. They had survived both the fire and another winter, and they were glad that spring had returned.

One warm morning Owl was again sleeping in his tree, snoring loudly and contentedly.

Through the brush Thumper and his four children ran, hopping onto the log under Owl's tree. Each of the rabbits began thumping on the log to get the sleeping bird's attention.

"Wake up! Wake up, friend Owl," called Thumper.

"Wake up, friend Owl!" the rabbit children called.

"Ohhh, what now," said Owl sleepily. "Hey, what's going on around here?"

But Thumper and his children were too excited to stay around and chat. Befuddled, Owl watched the rabbits dash through the woods.

Then Flower ran by, calling up to Owl, "It's happened!"

"Happened?" asked Owl, still confused.

"Yes," said the skunk. "In the thicket."

Flower looked behind and called to a tiny skunk who was following him. "Hurry up, Bambi!"

"Yes, Papa, I'm coming," said the little skunk named Bambi.

Everyone in the woods seemed to be heading toward the thicket. Pheasants ran along the ground. Above them, chipmunks and squirrels raced through the tall trees. Even a mole and his family joined the parade, as four bumps in the ground sped toward the thicket. On, above, and below the earth, everyone was heading to the same place.

In the thicket Faline was resting. All the animals crowded around, looking at her. The moles' heads popped out of their tunnels right in front to get the best view. Even sleepy Owl did not want to miss this moment, and he landed on a branch overhead.

"Ahhh," sighed the animals. "Oh my."

"Look!" said a raccoon. "Two of them."

Next to Faline were two spotted fawns. One fawn woke up, blinking as it looked at all the smiling faces watching it. The other fawn tried to get up on its long legs. But they were too wobbly.

"Well, sir," said Owl, "I don't believe I've ever seen a more likely looking pair of fawns."

Faline looked tenderly at her two babies. She thought they were so wonderful.

"Prince Bambi ought to be mighty proud!" said Owl.

Faline smiled and gazed up at the tall cliff above the thicket. She

could see Bambi standing against the sky. Next to him, his father stood proud, too. Then the old stag left, letting Bambi watch over the woods alone.

From the cliff Bambi could see his home—the forest that had survived, as he had, harsh winters and fire. These woods were his, and they were full of life again. He was the Prince of the Forest, and now there were new children to protect and care for, just as his mother and father had taken care of him.

Bambi looked down at the thicket where his beloved Faline lay near his two children. The sight of his family filled Bambi's heart with happiness and love. It was spring in the woods, and the joyful stag listened to birds chirping nearby. On this very special morning, their merry songs once more filled the woods with the wonderful news that life was beginning again.